This book belongs to

....

First published in 2018 by Miles Kelly Publishing Ltd
Harding's Barn, Bardfield End Green, Thaxted, Essex, CM6 3PX, UK

2 4 6 8 10 9 7 5 3 1

Publishing Director Belinda Gallagher
Creative Director Jo Cowan
Editorial Director Rosie Neave
Senior Editor Becky Miles
Design Managers Joe Jones, Simon Lee
Image Manager Liberty Newton
Production Elizabeth Collins, Caroline Kelly
Reprographics Stephan Davis, Jennifer Cozens
Assets Lorraine King

ISBN 978-1-78617-480-2

Printed in China

British Library Cataloguing-in-Publication Data
A catalogue record for this book is available from the British Library

Acknowledgements

The publishers would like to thank the following artists who have contributed to this book:
The Bright Agency: Maddie Frost (including decorative frames), Sarah Jennings

Made with paper from a sustainable forest

www.mileskelly.net

the race!" and he gave Daisy a rosette. Brave Princess Daisy had saved Prince Butterfingers and she had also won a race. She had quite forgotten her shyness. This was the best birthday party ever!

Butterfingers. They had both
fallen in the jelly castle
and were covered from
head to toe in sticky
pink jelly! Then
Daisy looked at
Prince Butterfingers,
and they both burst
out laughing.

Prince Theo ran
up to Daisy and
said, "You won

23

The Red Slippers

♥

The Princess and the Jelly Castle

Miles Kelly

The Red Slippers

Rosy-red was a sweet little girl, with beautiful brown eyes, soft pink cheeks and dark hair. Sadly her mother died the day Rosy-red was born so the little girl was cared for by her

grandmother, who loved her
dearly. On her first birthday
Rosy-red's father gave her
some red slippers. As Rosy-
red's feet grew, her red slippers
got bigger too, so they always
fitted her. No one knew that
the slippers were magic.

One day when Rosy-red
returned home from a walk in
the woods, she found that her
grandmother had gone. In the

house were three strangers.
"Who are you?" asked
Rosy-Red.

The Red Slippers

"I am your new mother," said one, "and these are your new sisters." Rosy-red's father had married again and his new wife had sent her grandmother away.

Rosy-red's new mother was mean to her. She made her fetch water from the well and carry the heavy bucket all the way home. Her sisters often shouted at her too. Rosy-red was sad, so she didn't wear her red slippers anymore.

Then one day, as Rosy-red lowered the bucket into the well, she sang, "Swing and sweep and don't stop until you come back up to the top."

A genie was sleeping at the bottom of the well and Rosy-red's song woke him. The genie loved her sweet song so much that he dropped some precious jewels into the bucket.

The Red Slippers

Rosy-red thought, 'If I give these jewels to my sisters maybe they will be kinder to me.' So she handed the jewels to her sisters and told them all about what happened at the well. But the sisters weren't happy, and they snatched the jewels and the bucket from Rosy-red.

The sisters ran to the well and as they lowered the bucket

they sang Rosy-red's
song. But the genie
didn't like their
croaky voices, so he
filled their bucket with
toads and frogs.

The sisters were
angry and threw
Rosy-red out of
the house. She
just had time to
put on her red

slippers, then she ran away into the woods.

After a while it began to get dark and Rosy-red was frightened. She saw a light in a cave, and an old woman invited her inside. It was Rosy-red's grandmother! Rosy-red was so tired that she soon fell asleep. When she awoke, she found that one of her red slippers was missing. "I must go and look for it," said Rosy-Red.

"You can't do that, a storm is raging," said her grandmother. So Rosy-red went back to sleep.

A little while later, Rosy-red was woken by a man's voice. The man had found a red slipper and he asked Rosy-red's grandmother if she knew who it belonged to. But grandmother was afraid that Rosy-red's stepsisters had sent him to find her. So she said she didn't know, and the strange man left.

The next day the man called again. He said, "I am a prince. I must find who this shoe belongs to." So Rosy-red bravely stepped out of her hiding place. She was wearing her one red slipper. The prince put the other red slipper on Rosy-red's bare

foot. "Let us get to know each other. If you like me, we will get married and you will be my princess," said the prince.

So Rosy-red left the cave
with her grandmother and the
prince. She spent many happy
days living in the prince's palace
and soon they were married.
And from then on she always
wore her magical red slippers.

The Princess and the Jelly Castle

Once upon a time there was a shy princess called Daisy who was scared of most things. So you can imagine how worried Princess Daisy was when the king and queen told her they were giving her a birthday party, and lots of other young princes and princesses were invited.

On the day of her party Daisy hid upstairs in her bedroom. She was too scared to meet her guests. The queen held Daisy's hand and they walked downstairs. Daisy looked beautiful in her sparkly purple dress and she wore a little purple and gold crown. But all the way to the garden, Daisy looked down at the ground, as she was too frightened to look up. "You're doing great," whispered her mother.

Fairy lights were hung around the garden and all the royal children wore their best clothes. By the pond was the biggest jelly castle you've ever seen!

"Come and play Pin the Tail on the Dragon," said Princess

Candy to Daisy. So Daisy shyly followed. Candy covered Daisy's eyes with a scarf, then spun her around. Daisy wasn't very good at the game and pinned the tail on the wrong end of the dragon. She thought the other children must *be* laughing at her and her face turned bright red.

Next Daisy tried the Golden Egg and Spoon Race. But she dropped the egg at the start

and quickly ran and hid behind
the king. "I'm not very good at
any of the games," she said.

"It doesn't matter. Just try
your best," said the king.

Then Prince Theo asked
Daisy to have a race with him.
But Daisy's knees were shaking
and she was too scared to
move. Just at that moment she
looked across the garden and
saw Prince Butterfingers

carrying a plate of sausages. He wasn't looking where he was going and he was walking towards the deep pond – and he couldn't swim!

Without thinking, Daisy ran as fast as she could across the garden and pushed Prince Butterfingers out of the way, just in time! Everyone at the party stopped talking and looked at Daisy and Prince